THE USBORNE
FIRST STORY BOOK

Retold by Heather Amery

Illustrated by Stephen Cartwright

Contents

Language Consultant: Betty Root

Cover Design by Non Taylor and Zöe Wray

There is a little yellow duck to find on every page of the stories

Notes for Parents

Fairy stories have a very long history; so long that we do not know when and by whom they were first invented. That they continue to survive is proof of their popularity with children of many generations and cultures.

The stories selected for this book are particularly helpful to young listeners and readers. The constant, natural use of refrains with events often repeated, enable children to enjoy the security of repetition and the pleasure of anticipation. Familiarity with the various characters in the stories helps children to identify with them and work through their own feelings of kindness, consideration, aggression, fear and frustration. The expectation of good being rewarded and evil punished is rarely unsatisfied.

In these Usborne versions, the spirit of the original story has been retained and the simple text and sensitive illustrations bring a real freshness to these favourite tales.

Fairy stories will continue to fascinate children of a wide range of ages; read this lovely book together, often.

Betty Root

This edition first published in 2000 by Usborne Publishing Ltd, 83-85 Saffron Hill, London EC1N 8RT, England.
UE Copyright © 2000, 1988 Usborne Publishing Ltd. The name Usborne and the devices ♀ ⊕ are Trade Marks of Usborne Publishing Ltd.

LITTLE RED
RIDING HOOD

Once upon a time, there was a little girl who lived with her mother on the edge of a big, dark forest. The little girl's Grandmother made her a bright red cloak with a hood. She was so pleased with it, she wore it whenever she went out, so everyone called her Little Red Riding Hood.

One day, her mother called Little Red Riding Hood into the kitchen.

"Your Grandmother is ill," she said. "I've put some food in a basket and you can take it to her. Go along the path to her cottage but, remember, don't talk to any strangers you meet on the way."

Little Red Riding Hood waved goodbye to her mother and went into the forest with the basket.

It was such a lovely sunny day, she sang a little song to herself as she skipped along the path. She did not see a big grey Wolf with gleaming eyes watching her from behind a tree.

Suddenly the Wolf jumped out in front of her. Little Red Riding Hood was frightened but the Wolf smiled at her.

"Where are you going, little girl?" he asked.

"I'm taking this basket of food to my Granny who lives in a cottage in the forest," she said.

The Wolf licked his lips and smiled.

"Why not pick some flowers for her?" he said.

Little Red Riding Hood did not like the Wolf's smile but she knew her Grandmother would like the flowers.

"That's a good idea, Mr Wolf," she said, politely.

She put down her basket and started to pick a big bunch of flowers. The Wolf watched her for a moment and smiled again, showing all his sharp white teeth. Then he ran silently down the path through the forest to find Grandmother's cottage. He was very, very hungry.

The Wolf found the cottage and looked through the window. Grandmother was sitting up in bed.

He knocked loudly on the front door.
"Come in," called Grandmother.
The Wolf opened the door and ran in. Quick as a flash, he gobbled her up in one great gulp.

Then he climbed slowly into Grandmother's bed
and put on her night cap and glasses. He pulled
the bed clothes right up to his chin and settled
down on the pillows.

"Little Red Riding Hood will soon be here," he
said to himself, and waited for her to come in.

When Little Red Riding Hood reached the cottage with her basket of food and bunch of flowers, she knocked on the door.

"It's me, Granny," she said.

"Come in, my dear," called the Wolf in a squeaky voice. "I'm in my bedroom."

Little Red Riding Hood opened the door.
"Hello Granny," she said. "I've brought you some food and flowers." Then she stared and stared. "But, Granny," she said, "what big eyes you've got."

"All the better to see you with," said the Wolf.

"But, Granny," said Little Red Riding Hood, feeling a bit frightened, "what big ears you've got."

"All the better to hear you with," said the Wolf, smiling at her.

"But, Granny," said Little Red Riding Hood, feeling very frightened, "what big teeth you've got."

"All the better to eat you with," growled the Wolf, and he jumped out of bed.

Little Red Riding Hood screamed but the Wolf gobbled her up in one great gulp. Then he climbed slowly back into bed, pulled up the bed clothes, gave a great yawn and fell asleep.

Out in the forest, a Woodman heard the scream.
"I wonder what that was," he said. "I'd better go
and see if the old lady is all right."

He ran as fast as he could to the cottage, rushed
in through the open door and straight into
Grandmother's bedroom.

When he saw the Wolf asleep in Grandmother's bed, he killed it with one mighty blow of his axe. Then he cut it open with his knife.

Inside were Little Red Riding Hood and her Grandmother, a bit squashed and crumpled, but alive and very happy to be rescued.

"Thank you very much for saving us from the wicked Wolf," said Grandmother. "Now he can never frighten anyone ever again."

The Woodman dragged the dead Wolf out of the cottage and they all sat down to a delicious meal.

THREE LITTLE PIGS

Once upon a time, there was a Mother Pig who had three baby Pigs and they all lived together in a tiny little house.

The baby Pigs grew and grew until, one day, Mother Pig said, "You're too big for my tiny house. It is time you had houses of your own."

Next day Mother Pig packed up a bundle of food for each little Pig and off they trotted down the road.

"Goodbye, dear children," said Mother Pig, waving to them. "Build your houses well and, remember, never open the door to the Big, Bad Wolf. He would like to eat you."

Soon the first little Pig met a man carrying a huge bundle of straw.

"Please, sir," said the Pig, "will you give me some straw so I can build a little house of my own?"

"Yes," said the man, and gave him a big bundle.

The little Pig began to build his house of straw. He worked very hard, and by the end of the day, he had finished his lovely little house. It had a big door at the front, a little door at the back, and two small windows.

"Now I will be safe and snug inside," he said.

The second little Pig trotted down the road and met a man carrying a huge load of sticks.

"Please, sir," he said, "will you give me some sticks so I can build a little house of my own?"

"Why, of course," said the man and he gave the little Pig lots of strong sticks.

All day the little Pig worked and worked. When he had finished, he had a lovely little house with strong walls, a roof, two doors, two windows and a chimney.

"This will keep the Big, Bad Wolf out," he said, "and I will be safe and snug inside."

The third little Pig trotted down the road and met a man with a huge load of bricks.

"Please, sir," said the little Pig, "will you give me some bricks so I can build a little house of my own?"

"Certainly," said the man and gave him a lot.

For days the little Pig worked and worked. He built the walls, put on the roof and fitted in the windows. When he had finished, he had a lovely little house with thick walls, a big chimney, two doors and two windows.

"I'm not afraid of the Big, Bad Wolf," he said.

One day, the Wolf knocked on the door of the straw house. "Little Pig, let me in," he said, "or I'll huff and I'll puff and I'll blow your house down."

"No, Mr Wolf, I won't let you in," said the Pig. So the Wolf huffed and puffed and he blew the house down.

The little Pig ran all the way to the stick house.

But soon the Wolf came knocking on the door. "Little Pig, let me in," he said, "or I'll huff and I'll puff and I'll blow your house down."

"No, no, Mr Wolf, we won't let you in," said the two little Pigs.

The Wolf huffed and puffed and blew the house down.

The two little Pigs ran as fast as they could all the way to the brick house. But soon the Wolf came knocking on the door.

"Little Pig, let me in," he said "or I'll huff and I'll puff and I'll blow your house down."

"No, no, we won't let you in," said the Pigs. So the Wolf huffed and puffed and puffed and huffed.

And he huffed and puffed and puffed and huffed but he could not blow the house down. He was very hungry and very out of breath. He prowled round and round the house, looking for a way in.

Then the Wolf jumped up on to the roof and looked down the chimney. The three little Pigs quickly lit a big fire in the stove and put a huge pot full of water on it.

''Now we're ready for the Big, Bad Wolf,'' they said, and waited for him.

The Wolf slid down the chimney and fell into the pot of water with a big splash. One little Pig quickly put the lid on the pot and another tucked in the Wolf's tail.

"That's the end of the Big, Bad Wolf," they said and the three little Pigs danced with joy.

"Now we'll have supper," said the third little Pig, "and you can both stay with me in my little brick house for ever."

After supper, the three little Pigs went to bed, safe and snug, and happy that the Big, Bad Wolf would never, ever frighten them again.

GOLDILOCKS
AND THE
THREE BEARS

Once upon a time, there was a family of three Bears who lived in a cosy little cottage in the middle of a big wood.

There was great big Daddy Bear, there was middle-sized Mummy Bear and there was tiny wee Baby Bear.

One morning, Mummy Bear filled three bowls with porridge for the Bears' breakfast, but it was much too hot to eat.

"We'll go for a walk in the wood while it cools," said Daddy Bear, and the three Bears went out of the cottage and closed the door behind them.

Just then, along came a naughty little girl called Goldilocks who was walking through the wood all by herself.

Goldilocks went up to the cottage and peeped in at a window. When she saw that there was no one at home, she opened the door and looked in.

On the table were the bowls of porridge. First she tried Daddy Bear's porridge. "Too hot," she said.

Then she tried Mummy Bear's porridge.
"Too cold," she said.
Then she tried Baby Bear's porridge.
"Just right," she said, and she ate it all up.

Goldilocks was so full of porridge, she felt very sleepy. First she tried sitting in Daddy Bear's chair. "Too hard," she said.

She climbed down and then tried sitting in Mummy Bear's chair. "Too soft," she said.

Then she tried sitting in Baby Bear's chair.
"Just right," she said, and started to go to sleep.
But, suddenly, there was a loud crack and a bang.
Goldilocks screamed and tumbled on to the floor
with a bump. She was so heavy, she had broken
Baby Bear's chair into little pieces.

Goldilocks was cross. She got up and looked in the bedroom. There were three beds. First she tried lying on Daddy Bear's bed. "Too high," she said.

Then she tried lying on Mummy Bear's bed. "Too low," she said.

Then she tried lying on Baby Bear's bed.
"Just right," she said. She pulled up the bed
clothes, snuggled down and yawned twice. She
was soon so fast asleep, she did not hear the three
Bears come back from their walk in the wood and
open the door of their cottage.

The Bears were hungry and wanted their
breakfast. Daddy Bear looked at his bowl.
   "Who's been eating my porridge?" he said, in
his great big voice. Mummy Bear looked at her bowl.
   "Who's been eating my porridge?" she said, in
her middle-sized voice.

Baby Bear looked at his bowl.

"Who's been eating my porridge?" he said, in his tiny wee voice. "And they've eaten it all up." And he began to cry.

"Never mind," said Mummy Bear, 'we'll soon make you some more."

Daddy Bear was very angry,
"Someone has been in our cottage," he
growled, and searched all round the room. Then
he stopped and looked at his chair.
"Who's been sitting in my chair?" he said, in his
great big voice.

Mummy Bear looked at her chair.

"Who's been sitting in my chair?" she said, in her middle-sized voice.

Baby Bear ran to his chair.

"Who's been sitting in my chair?" he said, in his tiny wee voice. "And they've broken it all up."

The three Bears went into the bedroom. Daddy Bear looked at his bed.

"Who's been sleeping in my bed?" he said, in his great big voice. Mummy Bear looked at her bed.

"Who's been sleeping in my bed?" she said, in her middle-sized voice.

Baby Bear ran to his bed and looked at it.
"Who's been sleeping in my bed?" he said, in
his tiny wee voice. "And, look, she's still in it."
Goldilocks woke up with a terrible fright and
when she opened her eyes, she saw the three
Bears standing round the bed, staring at her.

She screamed and jumped out of bed. She climbed out of the window and ran home through the wood to her mother as fast as she could.

The three Bears never, ever saw Goldilocks again and Goldilocks never, ever went walking in the wood on her own again.

RUMPEL-STILTSKIN

Once upon a time, there was a poor miller who had a very clever daughter. The miller was so proud of her that he was always boasting about her. One day he even boasted about her to the King. "Your Majesty," he said, "my daughter is so clever that she can spin straw into gold."

The King did not believe the miller but he loved gold. He commanded the daughter to come to his Palace and led her to a room with a spinning wheel and a pile of straw.

"Spin this into gold by morning, or you will die," he said. And he locked her in.

The daughter was very frightened. "I can't spin straw into gold," she said, and she cried and cried.

Suddenly the door crashed open and in came a funny little man.

"Here I am," he said. "Now, what will you give me if I spin the straw into gold for you?"

"I will give you my necklace," said the daughter, staring at him.

The funny little man went to the spinning wheel and started to spin. He worked away all through the night and, by morning, he had spun all the straw into fine gold thread. Then he disappeared.

When the King came in, he was surprised but very pleased to see all the gold. He led the daughter to a bigger room with a spinning wheel and a bigger pile of straw.

"Now spin this into gold by morning, or you will die," he said. And he locked her in.

The daughter sat down and cried and cried. But soon the door opened and in came the little man.

"What will you give me if I spin this bigger pile of straw into gold for you?" he asked.

"I will give you my ring," said the daughter, and the little man snatched it from her.

The little man went to the spinning wheel and began to spin. By morning, he had spun all the straw into gold. Then he disappeared.

When the King came in, he was more surprised and more pleased to see all the gold. But he was very greedy and wanted even more.

He led the daughter to a bigger room with an even bigger pile of straw.

"Spin this into gold by morning, or you will die," he said. And he locked her in.

The daughter sat down and cried and cried. But soon the funny little man came in.

"What will you give me if I spin this even bigger pile of straw into gold for you?" he asked.

"I have nothing left," said the daughter.

"Then promise to give me your first baby when you are Queen," said the little man. "That may never happen," she thought, but she promised.

The little man went to the spinning wheel and worked all night. Then he disappeared. When the King came in, he was delighted to see so much gold.

"Marry me and we will always be rich," he said to the daughter. Soon there was a grand royal wedding and she became a Queen.

When the Queen's first baby was born, she was very happy. She forgot her promise to the little man.

But, one day, he came in and reminded her. The Queen cried and cried until, at last, the little man said, ''If you can tell me my name in three days, you may keep your child.'' Then he disappeared.

All day and all night the Queen sat thinking of all the names she knew. And she sent messengers round the country to find lots of new ones.

Next day, when the little man came in, she said, "Is it Tom or John, or Henry?"
"No, you are wrong," said the little man.

On the next day, when the little man came in, she tried to think of different names.

"Is it Bandylegs or Crook-shanks or Bogglehead?" she asked.

"No, you are wrong," said the little man. "If you can't tell me my name tomorrow, I'll take the baby."

Next morning, a messenger came to the Queen.
"I have no more names for you," he said "but
when I was in the forest, I saw a funny little man.
He was singing, 'Soon the baby I will claim, for
Rumpelstiltskin is my name'."

"Oh, thank you," said the Queen, happily.

When the little man came in, she said, "Is your name Mick, or is it Nick, or is it Rumpelstiltskin?"

"Someone told you," the little man shouted, and he stamped so hard with rage, his foot went through the floor and he had to pull it out again. Then he ran away and he was never, ever seen again.

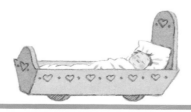

SLEEPING BEAUTY

Once upon a time, there was a good and wise King and Queen. But they were always very sad because they had no children.

At long last, after waiting many years, a baby daughter was born. The King and Queen were delighted and loved the little Princess very much.

When the baby Princess was christened, the
King and Queen gave a great feast at the Palace.
Six good fairies came but the King had forgotten to
invite the wicked, bad-tempered fairy whom no
one had seen for years. When she heard about the
feast, she was angry and thought up a wicked plan.

After the feast, the good fairies made wishes for the baby. When she grew up, they wanted her to be good, beautiful, clever, and to sing and dance.

The sixth good fairy was just about to make her wish, when the wicked fairy appeared, looking very cross. She had come without being asked.

"This is my wish for the Princess," she said. "When she is seventeen, she will prick her finger on a spinning wheel. Then she will die."

"Oh, no," cried the sixth good fairy. "I can't change that but my wish for her is that she won't die, but will go to sleep for a hundred years."

The King shouted and the Queen cried but the wicked fairy disappeared in a puff of smoke.

"Well," said the King. "I'll make a new law. All the spinning wheels in my kingdom are to be burned at once. If there are no spinning wheels, then the Princess can't prick her finger on one."

As the years passed and the Princess grew up, she became good, beautiful and clever, and she could sing and dance.

On her seventeenth birthday, there was a Grand Ball at the Palace, and the six good fairies came. Everyone had forgotten all about the wicked fairy.

The next day, the Princess found a little staircase in the Palace that she had never seen before.

When she pushed open the door, she saw an old woman sitting at a spinning wheel.

"Come in, my dear," said the old woman, who was really the wicked fairy.

"What are you doing?" asked the Princess. She had never seen a spinning wheel before.

"I'm spinning," said the old woman. "I'll show you how to do it. Come and hold this."

The Princess put out her hand.

"Oh, I've pricked my finger," she said.

In a second, the Princess was fast asleep.
Downstairs the King yawned, the Queen yawned
and everyone else yawned. Then they went to sleep.

The wicked fairy disappeared and the six good
fairies carried the sleeping Princess to her
bedroom and laid her gently on her bed.

In the Palace, nothing, not even a mouse, moved for a hundred years. Outside, a thick forest grew up all round it until only the roofs showed above the tree tops.

No one ever went near it except the good fairies, who watched over it while everyone slept.

After exactly one hundred years, a young Prince went hunting near the Palace. He saw the roofs above the trees and asked an old man about them.

"My Grandfather told me it's an enchanted Palace and there's a beautiful Princess asleep in there," said the old man. "But there's no way in."

The Prince thanked the old man and walked towards the Palace. But when he reached the trees they moved apart and let him through.

He ran up the Palace steps, past the sleeping guards and in through the open door. Nothing moved. It was so quiet, it was rather creepy.

The Prince searched the whole Palace and, at last, came to the Princess's bedroom. When he saw her lying asleep, he thought she was so beautiful, he bent over and kissed her very gently. The Princess opened her eyes and smiled at him.

"You have come at last," she said.

All over the Palace, everyone woke up, yawned, stretched, shook off the dust and started to talk and move about.

"I'm hungry," said the King. "Tonight we'll have a great feast." He thanked the Prince for coming to their rescue and the Queen invited him to stay.

Next day, the Prince asked the King if he might marry the Princess.

"Of course," said the King, and the Princess said, "Yes, please."

Soon there was a very grand wedding and the Prince and Princess lived happily ever after.

CINDERELLA

Once upon a time, there was a young girl called Cinderella. She lived in a big house with her father, who was often away from home, her horrid stepmother and her two nasty stepsisters. They hated her because she was pretty and because she was always kind and good-tempered.

The horrid stepmother and nasty stepsisters made Cinderella do all the work in the house. She cleaned and cooked from morning until bedtime.

They made her sit in the kitchen, gave her only scraps of food to eat and old clothes to wear. Her bedroom was in a cold, creepy attic.

One day, Cinderella and the two stepsisters
received invitations to go to a Grand Ball at the
Palace. The stepsisters screamed with excitement.
    "We must look our best for the Prince," one said.
    "We'll need expensive new dresses, and new
shoes, and new bags and gloves," said the other.

When the day came, they spent hours getting dressed and doing their hair. At last, when they were ready, Cinderella said, "Please may I come?"

"No, of course you can't. Stay in the kitchen," screamed the stepsisters, and off they went, slamming the door behind them.

Cinderella sat in the kitchen and cried. Then she heard someone say, "What's the matter, my dear?" She looked up and there was her fairy godmother. "I did so want to go to the Ball," said Cinderella. "Do just as I tell you," said her fairy godmother, smiling, "and you shall go."

"Now," she said, "bring me a big pumpkin from the garden, the cage with six white mice in it, the cage with a brown rat in it and six green lizards from behind the water tub."

Cinderella was very puzzled but she ran to fetch everything as quickly as she could.

When she brought them in, her fairy godmother tapped each one with her magic wand. And, as Cinderella watched, the big pumpkin turned into a wonderful coach, the six white mice into six white horses, the brown rat into a coachman, and the six lizards into six smart footmen.

Then the godmother tapped Cinderella's old clothes and shoes with her wand. In a twinkle, they turned into a lovely dress and shining glass slippers.

"Go to the Ball," she said "but, remember, you must leave before the clock strikes midnight."

"Oh, thank you, thank you," cried Cinderella.

Cinderella drove off in her coach and when she reached the Palace, the Prince came out to meet her. Everyone thought she was a Princess and even her nasty stepsisters did not recognize her. There was a grand supper with lots of delicious things to eat and drink, and musicians played all evening.

The Prince danced every dance with Cinderella and she was so happy, she forgot about the time. Suddenly she heard the clock striking midnight.

"I must go," she cried and ran as fast as she could out of the ballroom and down the stairs, losing one of her glass slippers on the way.

As she ran out of the Palace, the coach turned
into a pumpkin and her dress into her old clothes.

She ran all the way home in the dark and was
sitting in the kitchen when her stepsisters came back.
They told her all about the wonderful Ball and the
strange Princess who had suddenly run away.

Next morning, the Prince was very unhappy. He wanted to find the Princess but he did not even know her name. All he had was her slipper.

"I will search my kingdom for her," he said. "Every girl must try on the slipper, and when I find the one whose foot fits it, she shall be my bride."

For days, he went from house to house. Lots of girls tried on the slipper but it was too small for them.

At last, he came to Cinderella's house. The stepsisters tried to put it on. They pushed and they pulled, they cried and they screamed, but their feet were much too big.

Cinderella watched them. "May I try?" she said.
"No, you can't," shouted the stepsisters, angrily.
"Let her try," said the Prince, kindly.
Of course, the slipper fitted perfectly. At that
moment, her fairy godmother appeared and
Cinderella's old clothes turned into a lovely dress.

"I have found you at last," said the Prince.
"Please will you marry me?"

"Oh, yes," said Cinderella, happily.

"Oh, no," shouted the stepsisters, very crossly.

Soon the Prince and Cinderella were married.
They lived in the Palace and were happy ever after.